For Eddie, Lewis, Hayley, Jake, and Kate — A. H.

For Linda Lyall — M. M.

Text copyright © Anita Harper, 1987, 2007
Illustrations copyright © Mary McQuillan 2007
First published in Great Britain in 1986. This revised edition published in 2007
by Piccadilly Press Ltd., 5 Castle Road, London NW1 8PR, www.piccadillypress.co.uk.
This revised edition first published in the United States
by Holiday House, Inc. in 2007.
All Rights Reserved
Printed and Bound in China
www.holidayhouse.com
First American Edition
1 3 5 7 9 10 8 6 4 2

Library of Congress Cataloging-in-Publication Data

Harper, Anita.
It's not fair! / by Anita Harper ; illustrated by Mary McQuillan. — 1st American ed.
p. cm.
Summary: A girl cat, resenting the preferential treatment
enjoyed by her new baby brother, finds that she does
get to do some things he cannot.
ISBN 978-0-8234-2094-0 (hardcover)
[1. Babies—Fiction. 2. Brothers and sisters—Fiction.
3. Cats—Fiction.]
I. McQuillan, Mary, ill. II. Title.
PZ7.H2313Its 2007
[E]—dc22
2006037238

It's Not Fair!

by Anita Harper
illustrated by Mary McQuillan

Holiday House ● New York

When Mom and Dad brought
my baby brother home,
everyone fussed over him.

It wasn't fair!

"What about me?"
"You're a big girl now," my mom said.

I'm not **THAT** big.

People are always doing things for HIM.
I have to do things for myself.

It's not fair!

If he makes a mess, it's all right.

If I make a mess, I get into trouble.

That's not fair!

When we go out, I have to walk.

But my baby brother can ride.

It makes me MAD!

When the babysitter is here
and my brother screams,
she tries to find out what's wrong.

When I scream,
she tells me to be quiet.

It's not fair!

Now my brother's getting bigger.
The other day we went for a walk
in the rain. He wanted to walk,
but my mom wouldn't let him.

He didn't think
that was fair!

And when we go to the park,
he wants to slide down the hill,
but HE isn't big enough.

He doesn't think **THAT'S** fair either!

When I go to playgroup,
my brother wants to go too,
but he can't.

He doesn't think **THAT'S** fair at all.

Now when my friends come over,
my brother wants to play with us,

but he's too small.

He lets us know he doesn't think that's fair.

Sometimes I'm allowed to stay up late, but my brother has to go to bed.

He screams and screams, because
it's not fair!

My brother has started to talk now.
Today I'm going to a party
and he can't go.

Do you know what he said?
"It's not fair!"

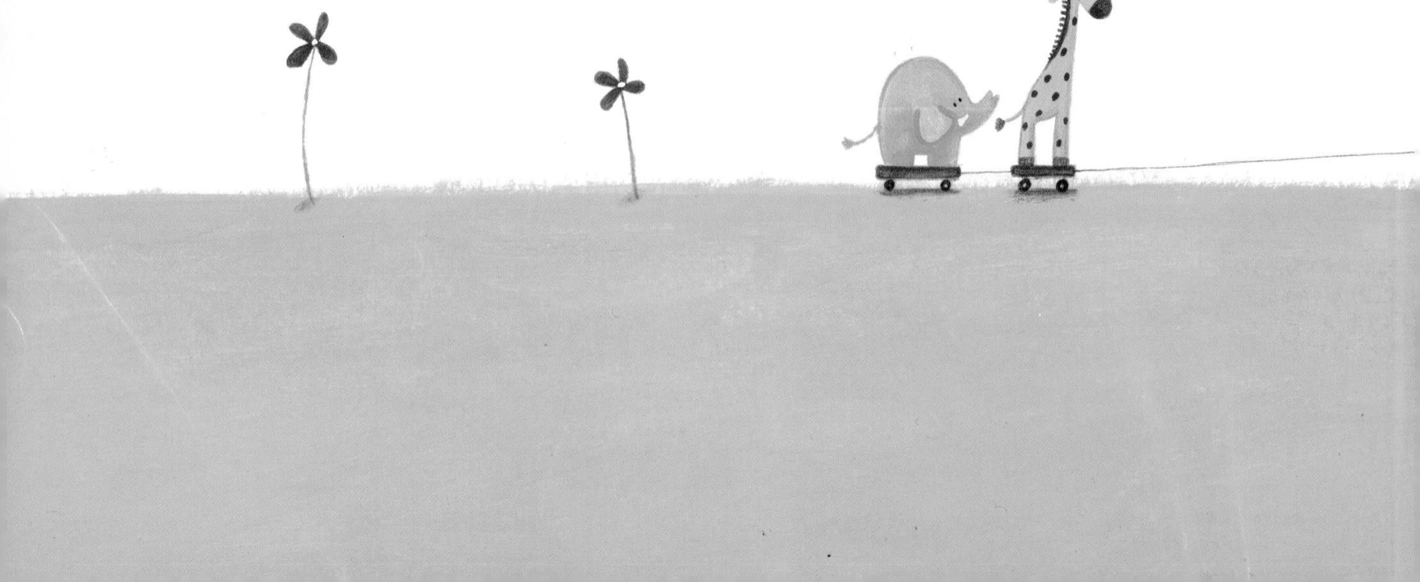